caillou®

My First Play

Adaptation of the animated series: Marilyn Pleau-Murissi
Illustrations: CINAR Animation; adapted by Eric Sévigny

chouette COOKIE JAR

Caillou was at day care playing dinosaurs with his friends, Clementine and Leo. Their teacher, Anne, came over to them. "Hello, dinosaurs. Do you remember what we are doing today?" Caillou, Clementine, and Leo looked at each other.

Then Caillou remembered.
"The play, the play!"
he exclaimed.
"That's right!" Anne said.
"YAY!" The children shouted.
"Okay, then let's get started."

There were so many costumes inside the trunk! Caillou and his friends wanted to try them all on. Caillou pulled out a huge red hat and said, "Look, I'm a pirate."
Leo found a clown's nose and Clementine put on a witch's hat.

"Remember for this play, we need specific costumes," Anne said. She reached into the trunk and pulled out a sun costume.
"Caillou, you chose the sun, Clementine, you're the flower; and Leo you were going to be a rain cloud?"

Anne helped the children dress and said,
"Now, we need a story."
"I'm a beautiful flower," Clementine said.
"Can you make the flower hot and thirsty,
Mr. Sun?" Anne asked Caillou.
Caillou stretched out his arms and Clementine
pretended to be very very thirsty.

Caillou, Clementine, and Leo laughed and played around. "Okay. Okay," Anne said. "But we need to practice properly. We want to be ready for when your parents arrive. Leo, we need the cloud now." Leo stepped forward and the children practiced all morning.

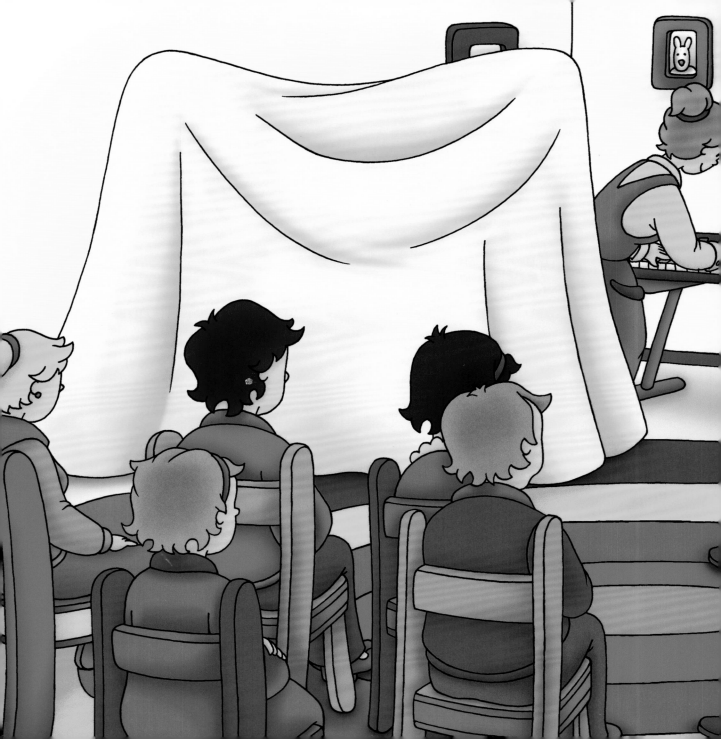

The parents arrived and were sitting in front of the stage. Behind the curtain, there was a lot of pushing going on.

"It's time... Shh... They're here... Ouch... Stop!"
You could hear Caillou, Leo, and Clementine talking.

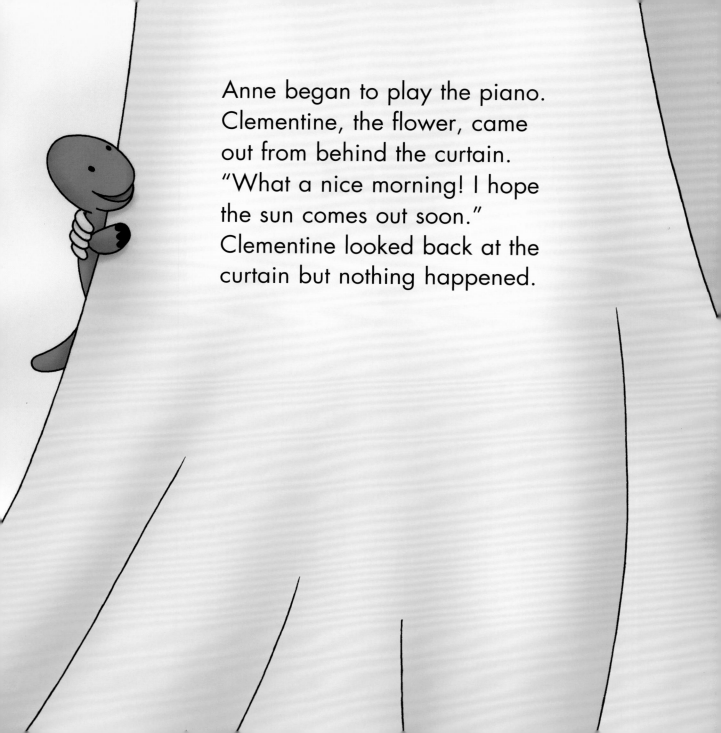

Anne began to play the piano.
Clementine, the flower, came
out from behind the curtain.
"What a nice morning! I hope
the sun comes out soon."
Clementine looked back at the
curtain but nothing happened.

Clementine repeated a little louder, "I hope the sun comes out soon!"
Caillou and Leo giggled behind the curtain.
"Oops, that's me," Caillou said suddenly and went out, waving his arms at the flower.
"Hello, beautiful flower, let me warm you up."

"Oh, the sun is making me so thirsty," Clementine sighed.

Then it was Leo's turn. The rain cloud appeared from behind the curtain and sprinkled water on the flower.

"Thank you, Mr. Cloud," said the flower.